HIGHWAY TRUCKS

Written by Justine Korman
Illustrated by Steven James Petruccio

SCHOLASTIC INC.
New York Toronto London Auckland Sydney

ISBN 0-590-02381-0

TONKA® and TONKA® logo are trademarks of Hasbro, Inc.
Used with permission.
Copyright © 1998 by Hasbro, Inc. All rights reserved.
Published by Scholastic Inc.

12 11 10 9 8 7 6 5 4 3 2 1   8 9/9 0/0 01 02 03

Printed in the U.S.A.   24
First printing, November 1998

Martha can't stop smiling. Today her dream is coming true. This is her first day as a trucker!

Martha has spent the last ten weekends going to Truck Driving School. She studied in a classroom and on the road. Martha learned about trucks and the trucking business, handling cargo, reading maps and signs, and driving under many different conditions. All her hours of hard work have led up to today!

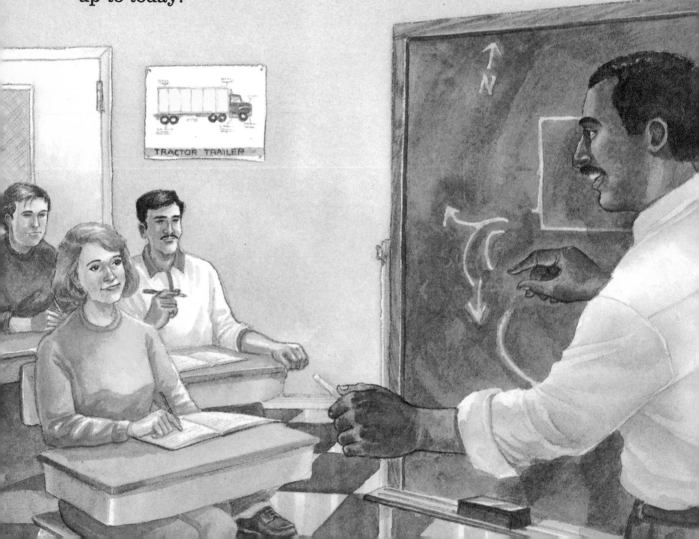

Martha backs her tractor up to her trailer. The tractor
section in the front of Martha's truck includes the engine
and the driver's cab. The trailer is a big box for holding
cargo. The tractor pulls the trailer like the engine of a
train hauling a freight car. A ring-shaped collar called the
coupling or fifth wheel links the two parts of Martha's
tractor trailer.

Martha's trailer is already loaded. Today she starts her cross-country journey, delivering books from a printing company in North Carolina to a warehouse in California. From the warehouse, other trucks will bring the books to schools, stores, and libraries.

Martha's dispatcher reviews the route. It's easy. Martha will take interstate highways all the way. A highway is a wide road designed for high-speed traffic. Numbered interstate highways cross the United States from north to south and east to west.

Martha is eager to get on the highway. She drives up to the entrance ramp and switches on her turn signal. Curly wires carry electricity between the tractor and the trailer, so the signal blinks at both the front and back of the truck. Other coils bring air to the brakes.

Martha looks over her shoulder to check for oncoming traffic. As she enters the highway, she glances in the wing mirror sticking out from the side of her cab. Martha sees a pickup truck coming up behind her. She pushes down the gas pedal to get up to highway speed before the pickup gets too close. Highway vehicles must maintain a safe distance — in case the front vehicle gets a flat tire or has to suddenly brake.

Soon, Martha moves into the left lane. Most trucks travel in the fast or through lane, leaving the right lane for slow and local traffic. Martha likes the view from her tall cab. Through the big windshield she can see far down the highway. There are many other trucks on the busy highway.

Trucks are often named for the number of wheels they have and how many of those wheels are powered by the engine. Martha's truck is an 18 x 6. Some of these 18 wheels are dual wheels. That means there are two tires on the same side of an axle. Dual wheels help trucks carry heavy loads.

Most of the smaller trucks Martha sees are rigid or straight trucks. Rigid trucks are one-piece, like a van.

Two-piece trucks like Martha's tractor trailer can be longer than rigid trucks because they can bend to make turns. Martha passes a refrigerated tractor trailer. This special truck keeps food cold on the way to the store.

Martha sees other trucks designed to carry one certain load, like logs, cars — or even houses! Most highway trucks open only in the back. But Martha spots one curtainsider. When the heavy, folding curtains are pulled back, big loads can be moved through the wide opening along this trailer's sides.

Martha's truck needs diesel fuel, not gasoline. Most trucks use diesel because it is more powerful and cheaper than gasoline. Martha takes out her logbook and looks at her watch. She records how much fuel she buys, how far she has traveled, and the time she is stopping for a break.

Seeing the tanker reminds Martha to check her fuel gauge. She decides to stop at the next filling station. The tanker stops at Diesel Dan's Truck Stop, too. Martha sees the driver attach a hose to the tanker's side. The hose carries gasoline to an underground storage tank beneath the gas pump.

Martha also sees a tanker carrying fuel. The tanker's curved sides are stronger than the straight sides of Martha's truck. The strong trailer protects the flammable liquid cargo. Inside, the tanker is divided into different compartments. These separate the gasoline from the diesel fuel. They also keep the tanker's liquid load from sloshing around enough to throw the truck off balance.

Flatbeds carry long loads like lumber. Low-slung lowboys are used to bring big construction vehicles to job sites. Martha passes a lowboy with a giant excavator for a passenger.

Martha needs to refuel, too. Luckily, truck stops are famous for good food. Some truck stops offer other services for truckers, like showers, video games, souvenirs, and even saunas! Martha likes talking to the other truckers. She leaves Diesel Dan's feeling alert and eager to be back on the road!

Martha follows the signs back to the highway. She knows that highway signs can tell a driver many things, like how many miles to the next exit or town and the fastest safe speed. Some signs warn of dangerous road conditions, like a steep slope or a sharp curve.

ROAD
WORK
AHEAD

Martha sees signs warning of road work ahead. She has to merge her truck into the slow lane. For the next few miles, there will only be one lane for traffic.

In the fast lane, road workers are repairing a pothole. An asphalt spreader pours out steaming asphalt. The steamroller waits to flatten the black, sticky mixture. Martha is glad to see the crew working to keep the highway smooth and safe.

But sometimes things go wrong on the highway. A family is moving. A rope on their truck comes untied. Suddenly, a plastic lawn chair flies off the truck bed at high speed!

Martha sees red brake lights flash on the car in front of her. Her foot quickly switches from the accelerator to the brake pedal. Compressed air travels along the coils between the tractor and the trailer. The air pushes the brake shoes against the brake drum. Martha's truck slows.

She looks around to see what's wrong. Martha sees the chair bounce into the next lane. All around Martha, vehicles swerve and slow down to avoid hitting the chair — and each other! Fortunately, none of the fast-moving vehicles collide.

If there had been a collision, a wrecker would have carried the disabled vehicles off the highway. Traffic never stops for long on a busy highway.

Wreckers aren't the only trucks that help during highway accidents. An ambulance is a rigid truck with emergency medical equipment. Ambulance drivers and attendants are trained to help people on their way to the hospital. They deliver medicine on the go!

Martha decides to take a break at the next rest stop. Rest areas along the highway give drivers a chance to stretch their legs, go to the bathroom, eat a snack, and focus their eyes on a pretty view, instead of miles and miles of yellow lines.

Martha enjoys the scenery. She also likes meeting the other travelers. One family is on their way to a dog show. Their truck has a kennel cage in the back to keep the dogs safely away from the driver. A retired couple is driving a camper to visit their grandchildren. Their rigid truck is a house on wheels!

Soon, Martha gets back on the highway. She drives until she almost reaches the ten-hour limit. Truckers are not allowed to drive more than ten hours in a day, to make sure they are alert behind the wheel.

Martha looks for a truck stop where she will
spend the night.

Soon, Martha is snugly tucked into the sleeper compartment of her cab. She feels tired, but happy. Today Martha is a trucker — and tomorrow the adventure will continue!

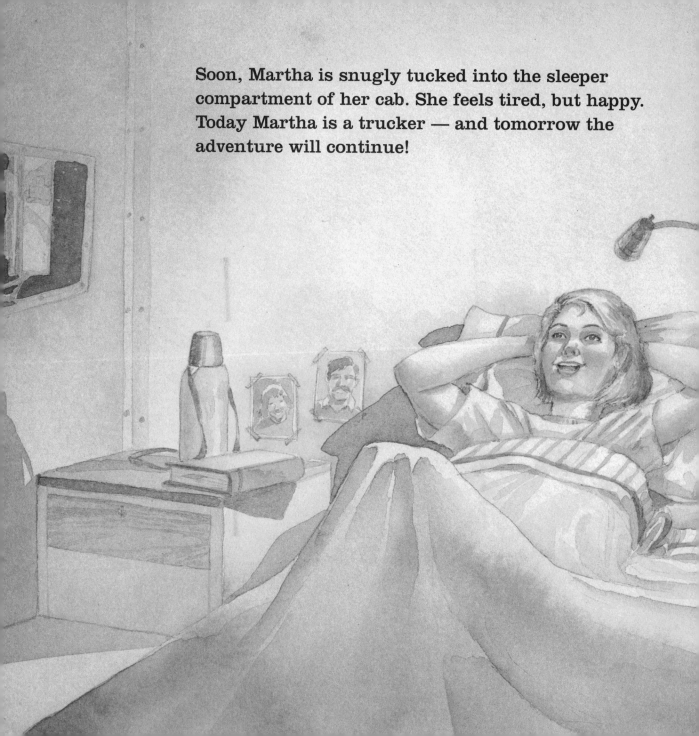